URIEN'S VOYAGE

Andre Gide

Urien's Voyage

Translated and with an Introduction and Notes
by Wade Baskin

THE CITADEL PRESS
New York

FIRST PAPERBACK EDITION 1964
PUBLISHED BY THE CITADEL PRESS
222 PARK AVENUE SOUTH, NEW YORK 3, N. Y.
MANUFACTURED IN THE UNITED STATES OF AMERICA
LIBRARY OF CONGRESS CATALOG CARD NUMBER 63-19701
COPYRIGHT © 1964 BY PHILOSOPHICAL LIBRARY, INC.

INTRODUCTION

Urien's Voyage was written at a critical period in
the life of André Gide and stands as a transitional but
prophetic work: the past lingers still in the face of an
uncertain future that is coming to birth. In later years
Gide was to look back on the period of its composition
as one of despair and to take a jaundiced view of the
product of his desperation. Here, as elsewhere, his
disclaimers bear close scrutiny, for he not infrequently
stresses a point not because of its inherent truth but
because of his desire for it to be true. The truth may
well be that he put much more of himself than he
realized in his early writings, and that readers familiar
with the most intimate of his later works, especially *Et
nunc manet in te,* will readily see that the experiences
and events chronicled here bear the stamp of the ir-
reconcilable tendencies that complicated his life from
pubescence to senescence.

Written at La Rocque during the summer of 1892,
Urien's Voyage complements three earlier works and
anticipates some fifty volumes still to come from his
pen. His previous works, two semi-autobiographical

books and a defense of the doctrine of symbolism, had revealed the three poles which alternately attracted and repelled him: religion, sex and art. Singly and collectively his writings yield substance for a fragmentary portrait of a haunted, lonely man, never quite sure of the Idea he was to manifest and forever vacillating between being moral and being sincere.

His early rigid Protestant and puritanical upbringing had created in him a conflict between his deeply religious yearnings and his intense sensuality. In the guise of Urien we find the mind and flesh of André. Plagued by doubts, discouraged over the prospect of having to choose between morality and sincerity, introverted and enthralled by his demon, Gide relapsed during the summer of 1892 into the solitary vice which was the bane of his existence. It was to save himself from the terror of madness and suicide that he began to compose the allegory that marks both his break with Symbolism and his gradual abandonment of the celibate life for the life of the flesh.

Earlier, the previous Christmas season at Uzès, in the south of France, in an excess of religious fervor, he had written that "all is vanity save knowledge of the Lord." Opposing this was the desire for self-manifestation in art, appropriately recorded on the last day of the year: "I am tormented by the fear of not being sincere." By Easter, we learn from his Journals (1892), he had turned away from creative writing in favor of learning. In his "wild lust for learning" he read Goethe, studied philology, and reveled in the joys of the mind. His sensuality waxes and wanes from one day to the next, with the result that he can on one day write of his desire to taste "the vanity of the other things" and to "exhaust their bitter flavor" and on another of his relapse into frenzied mysticism.

From his Journals we also learn that during the crucial summer spent at La Rocque, Gide almost lost his mind: "I was cloistered in my room . . . forcing myself to work; I was obsessed, haunted, hoping perhaps . . . through excess itself to exhaust my demon." He was to admit years later that he had put a great deal of himself into *Urien's Voyage* and that for those who could read between the lines the work was all too illuminating.

Urien's voyage is symbolic. Gide (Urien) and his companions set out on a voyage to find relief from their "bitter night of thought, study and theological ecstasy." Their voyage takes them from the "pathetic ocean" of the warmer latitudes to the "frozen sea" near the pole and provides Gide with a means of illustrating both the techniques and the credo of the Symbolist movement.

In a broad sense the Symbolist movement represents a flowering and a fulfillment of the ideals that inspired the earlier Romantic generations. Philosophically and esthetically viewed, it is a modern means of giving expression to a fundamental arrangement of the human mind; it puts stress on the intuitive rather than the rational, on the subjective rather than the objective, on freedom rather than restraint.

As formulated by Jean Moréas in an article published in *Figaro* in 1886, the doctrine of Symbolism was predicated on lofty aims and ambitions. Symbolist poets, whom others accused of being morbid and neurotic, were actually trying to create beauty, said Moréas. Beauty, according to the author of the abstract and verbose article later accepted as the manifesto of the Symbolists, was to be sought in "pure concepts" and "eternal symbols."

Five years later Gide defended the tenets of Symbolism in *Narcissus*. The views expressed in his treatise on Narcissus and illustrated in the allegory narrated by Urien may be summarized in these words: Visible forms are but the transient external symbols of eternal truths; the true poet sees beyond mere appearances (phenomena), grasps the Ideas (noumena) which they represent, and uses the former to suggest the latter; each man is born to make manifest an Idea—the truth, whether good or bad, which is his inmost self. Gide's problem was to conciliate sincerity to the Idea that he was to represent with morality.

The temptations, suffering, and surroundings of Urien and his companions are described with such profusion of detail that the reader can recreate them in their entirety, yet the pilgrims are never certain of the reality of either their experiences or their surroundings. The chimerical shores and crags that drift by their ship in the pathetic ocean are scarcely more chimerical than the "real" world was to Gide when he remarked in his Journal (in June, 1891) that things seemed to cease to exist for him when he "stopped thinking about them."

We note too that the crewmen made the mistake of confusing "passing things" with "eternal isles" while Urien and his companions, bending over the water like Narcissus (who saw both his own reflection and the moving panorama of life), realize that things reveal themselves through their changing aspects.

Various temptations which Urien resists, the stagnation of the Sargasso Sea, the voyage through the frozen sea, and the agony of despair after a futile search—all this is easy to interpret. Urien's resistance in the face of diverse temptations is the repressed side of Gide's own nature while the sensuous details with which he embellishes the most trivial item betray his recognition of physical desire as the ridiculous counterpart of piety. The stagnation of the Sargasso Sea has as its counterpart the physical excesses that brought Gide to the verge of madness during the summer of 1892. The passage through the frozen sea and the march to the polar regions are his quest for conquest of the world of the senses and attainment of the realm of the spirit.

Urien's Voyage is perhaps more important because of what it suggests than what it says. Readers familiar with Gide's later writings—especially his Journals and *Et nunc manet in te*—will find in this early allegory the elements that were to motivate the works of his maturity. "Without sensuality, sexuality and pride there could be no work of art," he later wrote. It is somewhat ironic that he made his supreme effort to dominate or sublimate his passions through art—and of course failed—when these very passions were at their peak. For though later when tortured by desire he prayed that he might no longer be enslaved by his flesh, even in old age he longed to remain "carnal and desirous until death."

Viewed against the background of his other works, the unpolished declamations of his youth may be more revealing than the carefully wrought images of his maturity. We might not be far from the mark if we concluded that during the last years of his life he achieved the ideals formulated during the first, realizing thereby the perfect life defined by Valéry, whom he was fond of quoting: "a dream of youth brought to fruition in maturity."

*　*　*　*

I have tried through occasional notes to call attention to relevant biographical details or statements from Gide's other writings. A more ambitious undertaking would probably illuminate the substratum of superstitions, myths and legends on which Gide erected his art. Names, numbers, episodes, events and a host of striking metaphors suggest a skillful blend of ingredients drawn from diverse cultures—Hellenic, Roman, Celtic, Germanic, Christian and Moslem, to name only the most obvious. It is my hope that the suggestions made here and in the notes that follow will stimulate further interest in this work and in its place in Gide's art.

In more than a few instances I have borrowed freely from Harold March's exemplary work, *Gide and the Hound of Heaven* (University of Pennsylvania Press, 1952). I wish also to acknowledge my indebtedness to my colleagues whose efforts are reflected in the foregoing remarks and in the translation of Gide's allegory: Dr. Margaret C. O'Riley, Professor Mildred Riling, and Mrs. Helen Scroggins.

WADE BASKIN

Southeastern State College

URIEN'S VOYAGE

I

When the bitter night of thought, study and theological ecstasy came to an end, my steadfast soul,
tortured since nightfall by loneliness, sensed the
approach of dawn and stirred uneasily. Without my
noticing it, my lamp had gone out; my casement had
opened to the dawn. I moistened my brow with the
dew from the panes, and relegating to the past my
spent revery, I gazed toward the dawn and ventured
into the narrow vale of metempsychoses.*

Dawns! Dreams of memories of maritime wonders
and oriental splendors which by night infused our
wearisome study with longing for travel! Long had I
wandered as if in a dream through a tragic valley,
searching for exotic breezes and sounds, when finally
I was overjoyed by the sight of towering rocks and a
blue sea.

* The similarity between the opening paragraph of the allegory
and the first scene in *Faust* is not surprising in view of the influence which Goethe exerted on Gide during the period of the composition of *Urien's Voyage*. [All notes are by the translator unless
otherwise specified.]

O sea eternal, I thought, shall we sail across these waves to our unknown destiny? Will our tender souls test their valor?

Awaiting me on the shore were my fellow pilgrims; I recognized them all but without knowing whether I had seen them somewhere before; our virtues were the same. The sun had already risen high above the sea. They had arrived at dawn and were watching the waves rise. I excused myself for being late; they forgave me, thinking that I had been detained along the way by certain dogmatic subtleties and scruples; then they reproached me for having reservations about consenting to come. As I was the last one and they were expecting no one else, we made our way toward the town with the great port where ships weigh anchor. Loud noises that emanated from there came to us on the shore.

The town that was to be our place of embarcation in the evening was vibrating from the sunshine, from loud noises and sounds of merry-making, from the white heat of high noon. The marbled quays burned our sandals; the festivities offered a medley of colors. Two ships had arrived the previous day, one from Norway and the other from the enchanting Antilles; and the crowd was hurrying to view the arrival of a third, a majestic ship, as it came into the port. It came from Syria, laden with slaves, nuggets, and bales of purple. There was much hurrying and scurrying on the deck; shouts of the crew were heard. From the top of the masts some sailors were loosening cords

while others, near the waves, were throwing out rope
the folds of flattened sails were hanging from the mai
yards, where oriflammes were displayed. The sea, o
the shoreward side, was not deep enough to allow th
ship to approach the quay; boats went out to the shi
and first brought back the slaves; and as soon as the
had been set ashore, the people scurried to see them
they were beautiful and almost naked, but sad. Th
sailors also placed perfumes and precious fabrics i
the boats, but they cast into the sea the bales of purpl
these were cheap goods; the waves carried them alon;
side dikes, where men were bending over with pole
to guide them toward the stairway. From the Antille
had come rare weeds, variegated birds and shells tha
relayed the sound of the waves on these happy shores
There was haggling as they were auctioned off; th
bazaars were cluttered with cages; some birds, mor
delicate than the others, were set loose in large cages
people paid to enter; all the birds sang, and merchant
added to the confusion. Jugglers and mimics per
formed in improvised stalls. On a stage cavorting
mountebanks tossed back and forth daggers and pen-
nants.

Farther away were the town's ice-houses which were
supplied by the Norwegian vessels returning with their
rimy cargos. Some cellars were very deep, but all had
been replenished, and this ship was unloading its
burden on the deck. A mountain was rising, green,
diaphanous and cool; thirsty sailors were coming there
to enjoy its shadow and to put their burning hands and

lips against its moist exterior. Saffron-skinned men in blood-stained cotton breeches were still carrying loads of snow on sagging boards and chunks of pure ice that they had recovered from the sea; snow and pieces of ice were being cast overboard; snow, ice and foam were borne along with the purple on the blue water which turned almost violet as waves dissolved the purple.

And now came the evening; the crimson sun was hidden by the cordage; crepuscular sounds arose; and in the becalmed port rocked the fabulous vessel that was to bear us away! Then, since this day had given us a foretaste of all that the future held in store, we ceased to look back and turned our eyes to the future; and the extraordinary ship, leaving behind it the port, the fair and the sunken sun, plunged into the night toward dawn.

II

Night at sea. We have been discussing our destinies. The night is clear; the *Orion* is sailing between two islands. The moon lights the cliffs. Blue sharks have come into view: the night watch called attention to them and to some dolphins; they were playing in the moonlight; near the sharks, they submerged and did not reappear; blue rocks glow dimly beneath the waves. Luminous jellyfish rise slowly from the deep and blossom in the night air, tossed by the waves like sea-flowers. The stars are dreaming. Leaning over the bow of the ship, near the cordage and above the waves, we turn our backs to the crew, to our companions, to all that is being done, and we look at the waves, the constellations and the islands. "We are watching the isles passing by," say the crewmen, who are somewhat contemptuous of us, as they forget while looking at each other that they are moving while these things are motionless and unaffected by our passing.

Changing aspects of massive cliffs, elongated promontories that vanish from sight! Precipitous banks! Metamorphoses of mountains! We know now that you remain; we look upon you as transient because we are moving; your aspect changes in spite of your constancy as we sail by. The night watchman calls attention to ships. We, leaning over the waves from dusk to dawn, learn to distinguish transient things from the eternal isles.*

That night we talked about the past; none of us knew how he had managed to come to the ship, but no one regretted the bitter night of meditation.

"From what obscure sleep have I awakened?" asked Alain. "From what tomb? I never stopped thinking and I am still sick. O becalmed, oriental night, will you at last bring relief to a tired brain obsessed by thoughts of God?"

"I was tormented by a desire for conquest," said Paride; "I paced my room, valiant but sad, and more exhausted by dreams of heroic acts than by their performance. What conquests lie before us now? what noble deeds? where are we going? Tell me! Do you know where this ship is taking us?" Not one of us knew, but all of us trembled on sensing our courage.

"What are we doing here," he continued, "and what just what is this life if the other one was our sleep?"

"Perhaps we are living our dream as we sleep in our rooms," said Nathanael.

---

* "My kingdom is not of this world," is the Gospel statement that most impressed Gide. He could never manage to believe completely in the real world which always seemed "somewhat fantastic" to him, nor in eternal life. He did believe "in another facet of this life, which escapes our senses."

"Or perhaps we're searching for regions to satisfy our souls," said Mélian.

But Tradelineau shouted: "Without a doubt, the fallacy of using vain logic and believing that you can do a thing well only if its causes are known, still enslaves you and motivates this pointless discussion. Why try to imbue our presence on the *Orion* with highly mysterious motives? We left our books because they bored us, because an unconscious remembrance of the sea and the real sky destroyed our faith in study; something else existed; and when warm, balsamic breezes came to stir the curtains on our windows, we descended willy-nilly toward the plain and began our journey. We were tired of thought, we wanted action; did you see how our souls turned joyous when, taking from the rowers their heavy oars, we felt the liquid blue resist! Oh, the *Orion* will surely carry us to distant shores. The spasms of courage that we experience will of themselves elicit feats of valor; let's hope for the best as we wait for our glorious destinies to unfold."*

That night we also spoke of the tumultuous town where we had embarked, of its fairs and of the crowd.

"Why keep thinking about those people whose eyes saw only things and who were not even astounded?"

* Two previous works (*Narcissus* and *André Walter*) reveal Gide's views on art and the relation of art to the two other poles which alternately attracted and repelled him—sexuality and religion. In the present work he effectively combines the three elements deemed essential for any work of art—sensuality, sexuality and pride.

said Angleval. "I liked the way Bohordin was sobbing during the circus acts; everything should be done as a rite; those people were watching the performances unceremoniously."

"What do you think of all this, Urien?" Angaire asked me.

And I replied: "One must always represent."*

Then, since the discussion was becoming unbearable for all of us and since thinking exhausted us, we promised not to speak further of the past or argue about things. Morning was approaching; we parted to sleep.

We had lost sight of the coasts and had been sailing on the open sea for three days when we came upon these beautiful floating islands that a mysterious current had been moving toward us for a long time. And our parallel flight in the midst of the incessantly agitated waves at first made us think the *Orion* motionless, stranded perhaps on the sand, but our illusion vanished when we examined the islands more closely. A boat brought us down to one of them; they were all almost identical and equally spaced. Their regular shape made us think that they were madrepores; they would undoubtedly have been quite flat without the luxuriant and magnificent vegetation that covered

* According to the Symbolists a man is born to make manifest an Idea. Gide wanted to represent, to manifest to others his truth which was his inmost self. His task was complicated by his inability to conciliate morality with sincerity in his own life.

them; toward the front the slightly uneven coral reefs, wherever their roots were exposed, were as gray as volcanic stones; toward the rear they floated like tresses, their roots reddened by the sea. Trees of unknown species, exotic trees bent under the weight of heavy bindweeds, and delicate orchids blended their flowers with the leafage. These were sea-gardens; flights of insects followed them; pollen trailed along on the waves.

The impenetrable underbrush forced us to walk along the edge of the shore, and often, when branches overhung the water, to crawl between them, clutching roots and vines.

We wanted to remain to the rear for a while and watch the huge insects fly, but the stifling perfumes that arose from the whole island and were carried to us on the wind, the perfumes that were already making our heads swim, would have killed us, I believe. They were so dense that we could see the aromatic dust spiraling upward.

We made our way to the other shore; startled pink flamingos and ibises took flight. We sat down on a coral rock; wind from the sea wafted the perfumes away from us.

The island must not have been very thick, for beneath it, in the deep sea, under the shadow that it cast, we could again see the light. And we thought that each such island must have become detached, like a ripened fruit from its stem; and when they were no longer held fast to the natal rock by anything, then, like insincere actions, they were at the mercy of the waves, borne along by every current.

On the fifth day, to our regret, we lost sight of them.

As soon as the sun had set, we bathed in water that was pink and green; and, since it reflected the sky, it soon became reddish brown. The warm, pacific billows were soft but penetrating. The oarsmen were awaiting us. We climbed back into the boat just as the moon was rising; there was a slight breeze; tacking our sails, we forced the boat into the wind. And sometimes we saw clouds, mauve-colored still, and sometimes the moon. In the silver wake that it left on the calm sea, the oars dug eddies of light; before us, in the wake of the moon, the *Orion* moved along, mysterious. The moon appeared first behind a mast, then alone—then by morning it had again fallen into the sea.*

* Gide's early works, written under the influence of the Symbolist movement, reflect not only his acute sensitivity but his belief in the supremacy of art over other means of cognition or expression. The Symbolists stressed the fusion of sensations and the use of concrete phenomena to suggest Ideas. From his earliest writings we learn that Gide in his solitary walks felt that "The landscape was but a projected emanation of myself . . . I created it step by step as I became aware of its harmonies . . . and I marveled as I walked through my dream-garden."

III

On the seventh day we came upon a sandy shore interrupted by arid dunes. Gabiler, Agloval, Paride and Morgain went ashore; they kept us waiting for twenty hours; they had taken leave of us around mid-day, and we saw them returning the following morning, running and gesticulating. When they were quite near, Paride shouted to us:

"Let's go," he said. "There are sirens on the island and we have seen them."

After they had caught their breath, while the *Orion* was sailing at full speed, Morgain related:

"We had walked all day among the blue thistles on the shifting dunes. We had walked all day without seeing anything but the hills that loomed before us, their crests wavering in the wind; our feet were burned by the sand, and the flashing dry air parched our lips and made our eyes smart. (Who can describe your pomp and plenitude, suns of the East, suns of the South on these sands!) When evening came, having reached the foot of a high hill, we felt so tired. . . .

We slept in the sand, without even waiting until the sun had set.

"We did not sleep long; the coldness of the dew awakened us long before the dawn. During the night the sands had shifted, and we no longer recognized the hill. We set out once again, climbing always, without knowing where we were going, whence we had come, where we had left the ship; but soon behind us appeared the light of dawn. We had reached a very wide plateau—at least it seemed to us very wide at first—and did not realize that we had traversed it until suddenly the plateau ceased and there opened before us a mist-filled valley. We waited. Soon the light of dawn appeared behind us, and as the sun rose the mists disappeared.

"Then it appeared, this prodigious city, not far from us in an immense plain. It was a gold-colored Moslem city with fantastic minarets; flights of stairs led to hanging gardens and, on terraces, mauve palms swayed. Above the town hovered fog banks penetrated by pointed minarets. The minarets were so high that the clouds remained imprisoned by them, looking for all the world like oriflammes, like oriflammes fully distended, without a wrinkle, in spite of the fluid air untroubled by the slightest breeze.

"Such, then, is our uncertainty: before high cathedrals we used to dream of mosque towers; before the minarets today, we dreamed of church steeples, and in the morning air we waited for the angelus. But in the still too cool dawn there was no sound save the unknown tremors absorbed by the empty air; suddenly with the appearance of the sun, a chant went up from a minaret, from the minaret nearest the rising sun—a strange, pathetic chant that almost made us weep. The voices quavered on a piercing note. A new chant resounded, then another; and one by one the mosques awoke melodiously as each was struck by a ray of sunlight. Soon all resounded. It was an uncanny plea brought to an end by a burst of laughter only to begin anew. Like larks, the muezzins answered each other in the dawn. They proffered questions followed by other questions, and the tallest, on the tallest minaret, lost in a cloud, said nothing.

"The music was so wonderful that we were spellbound, enraptured; then, as the voices became lower and softer, we wanted to draw nearer, unconsciously attracted by the beauty of the town and by the moving shadows of the palms. The voices became lower and lower; but as they fell, the city, staggering with the strophe, moved away from us and disintegrated; the slender minarets and palms disappeared; the stairway crumbled; through the discolored terraces of the gardens we saw the sea and the beach. It was a fleeting mirage that fluctuated with the chant. The chant ended, and this marked the end of the spell and of the fanciful city. Our frightfully constricted hearts had seemed on the verge of death.

"A vanishing vision tottering on a trill, a gasping for breath—and then we saw them lying on the seaweeds; they were sleeping. Then we fled, shaking so violently that we could hardly run. Happily we were quite near the ship; we caught sight of it behind a promontory: it alone separated you from the sirens. How dangerous it would have been for you if they had been able to hear you—and we dared not shout until we were quite near you for fear that the noise would awaken them. I don't know how we managed last night to walk so far and advance so little; I believe now that we marked time while these moving hills changed positions under our feet and that this plateau, this valley were but the effect of the spell cast by the sirens."

They tried then through discussion to determine how many sirens there were and marveled over their having escaped from the wily creatures.

"But tell us," said Odinel, "what were they like?"

"They were lying in the sea-weeds," said Agloval, "and their glowing green and brown tresses, which covered them entirely, blended with the vegetation around them; but we ran away too quickly to see them distinctly."

"They had webbed hands," said Cabilor, "and their steely, scaly thighs glistened. I ran away because I was terrified."

"I thought they were like birds," said Paride, "like giant red-billed sea-birds. Didn't they have wings?"

"O no! no!" said Morgain. "They were just like women, and very beautiful. That's why I ran away."

"But their voices, their voices! Tell us, what were

their voices like?" (And each one vowed that he had heard them.)

"They were like a shaded valley and cool water to the sick," said Morgain.

Then each spoke of the nature of the sirens and of their charms; Morgain fell silent and I understood that he regretted the sirens.

We did not bathe that day for fear of them.

IV

It was the thirteenth day; on this plain where we had been lost since morning, constantly walking but never knowing the route, we were beginning to become bored when we met a young girl. Stark naked in a field of alfalfa and still awaiting nubility, the dark lass guarded placid dromedaries. We asked directions of her; weeping, she pointed to the town.

. . . One hour later we saw the town; it was large but dead. We were gripped by a solemn sadness; for the ruined mosques, with their broken minarets, the great walls reduced to rubble, the columns, gave to this city a forlorn, monumental appearance. The broad street that we were following as we made our way over piles of debris finally disappeared in the countryside, under some almond-trees, near some abandoned marabouts.

For still another hour we walked. The plain came to an end; a hill appeared, which we climbed. At the top of the hill could be seen a new village. We walked through the streets; all the houses were closed; and for some unknown reason, we could see no one. Angaire said that, perhaps, the residents were working in the fields. The stifling heat that fell on the street from the yellow walls was unbearable. Big flies vibrated in the sun against the white doors. In front of one door, seated on the threshold, a child fondled his hideous phallus. We left the village.

The open land again stretched out before us. For another hour still we walked through the heat and dust. A square monument suddenly and inexplicably emerged on the landscape and shouts coming through an open door attracted us from a considerable distance. We quickened our steps, thinking that we would finally see something. We entered a vast room. A large crowd raised such a clamor that we were at first dumbfounded. We wanted to speak, to ask questions, but no one was listening and everyone, with frenzied gestures, pointed and looked toward the middle of the room.

Standing with our backs to the wall, we were able to see, in the center of the crowd, two howling dervishes beginning their ecstasy. They turned slowly to the sound of music produced by four squatting men but not heard because of the shouts of the crowd; and periodically, at the end of a musical couplet, they released a very high guttural howl to which the crowd responded with an enthusiastic stamp. Aside from headdresses half the height of their bodies, they wore only long, very wide robes. As the music urged them on, they began to whirl more rapidly; their robes fanned out and revealed their feet as they leaped about in their sandals; as they whirled more rapidly still, they threw off their sandals and danced barefoot on the stone floor; their robes spreading out and rising, exposed their pivoting legs; their headdresses tilted at an angle and their beards became unbearable to see; they slavered and their eyes were white with joy. The crowd went out of control and oscillated as if drunk. Then the dervishes became frantic and, screaming wildly, whirled at such a dizzying speed that their robes, stiffer than ever, became almost horizontal, revealed them stark naked, obscene. . . . We departed.*

And again we were in the open; it was evening. For an hour we walked, then we found the ship once more.

The sailors bathed in the warm water; the searing air dried their skins. Evening came, but without the coolness that brings repose; without the coolness of night like a kiss on the eyelids. The night is now so warm that we can not sleep. Silent flashes brush the edge of the sky, and on the waves vaguely appear fluorescent streaks. Half recumbent on the deck, sailors and cabin-boys are dreaming; and in the mysterious night, the dreamers stretch forth their arms and writhe in desire. We, however, have remained standing, for

* Gide was never able to divorce the sexual and the obscene. This passage recalls an episode in the life of the central figure in Gide's autobiographical *André Walter*. André derived ecstatic pleasure from piercing melodies, profusions of colors, and sudden metamorphoses; in a nightmare *she* suddenly threw her skirt over her head, and under it there was nothing at all.

we dared not lie down, and all night we heard their sighs blend with the sonorous breath of the sea. But our aloofness changed to concern as the calm of night descended upon our countenances.

V

On the twenty-first day we stopped opposite a shore covered with trees. Not far from the shore, we could see a town; leading to it was an avenue lined with myrtles, along which strolled groups of women; on both sides of the avenue, between the trees, canvas trestles and booths had been set up for a market, and from the ship we could see splotches of red and yellow representing sweet peppers and clusters of bananas.

Before the day's end, Mélian, Lambègue and Odinel went ashore, as did a part of the crew, to buy food and to ask directions. We waited for them all evening. The next day, Mélian, Lambègue and Odinel came back, but with only a few of the sailors. They were pale and their wide eyes sparkled with ineffable sweetness. They brought back admirable fruits, scarlet and bleeding like wounds, and cakes made from unknown ingredients; but when we tried to question them, they pretended extreme fatigue and stretched out in their hammocks; then we understood that they had been with the women on the coast, and we were extremely sad. Since we did not wish to set out again until all the others returned, toward evening Lambègue, Odinel, and Mélian, and those sailors who had returned with them the previous day, decided to revisit the town; we were unable to stop them; nor could we keep Alfasar and Hector from following them. Both of them must have talked with those exhausted by their nocturnal orgies, for we saw them standing for a long time beside their swaying hammocks.

All of them returned the following day, and the *Orion* managed once again to set sail. They had brought back fresh fruit—huge, purple fruit that looked like egg-plants; their eyes were haggard and insulting; their lips betrayed an ironic smirk. It was over the beautiful fruit that the quarrel began; they insisted that we taste it, but its sheen, its splendor made us suspicious of it; when we voiced our distrust, they made fun of us:

"Just look at you courageous gentlemen! You dare not even taste the fruit; you are afraid, and your sterile virtue springs from abstinence, from doubt. Will you always be dubious? Why?"

And without our asking, they related what they had done in town: the market, the purchase of the fruit, and the unknown tongue spoken by the women; then the lighted pleasure gardens and the lanterns in the foliage; they had remained there for a long time before entering, viewing the dances and girandoles through fences; then some passing women had taken them inside, and they had suddenly felt their resistance crumble at the touch of the women's hands. They had at first been ashamed, then had derided their shame. But when they tried to tell us about their nocturnal embraces, Angaire shouted out that he did not understand how any one dared to pair off to engage in these indispensable but filthy practices, and that at such moments he even shunned mirrors. *

His sudden candor caused an uproar. Angaire then said that he liked women only when veiled, and that he was afraid even then that they would become lewd and remove their garments at the first sign of tenderness. Then they burst out laughing and turned away from us. From this day on, we were no longer all united in our thought— and, acutely aware of what we did not wish to be, we began to know what we were.

They bathed in sad, blue water; they swam in the salty spume. Back in the boat, still naked for a long time, they watched their skin gleam with unwonted paleness and let the clear sea foam dry on them from the heat. And we were ashamed for them, for they looked very beautiful and seemed happier than mere men.†

* Paul Claudel called attention to Gide's fascination by mirrors and labeled his Journal "a series of poses . . . a monument of insincerity." During his early years Gide liked to stand before a dresser alternately writing on the table and looking at himself in the mirror.

† Gide in his intimate writings frequently called attention to his personal predicament and called his failure to achieve a blending of the spiritual and the sensual, one of the most bitter realities of his life.

We were not very fond of Alfasar, for he was pompous and choleric, but we regretted Mélian, who was gracious and compassionate.

VI

All day long beautiful slopes loomed before the ship; pink ibises and flamingos were fishing for crabs along the sandy shore. A little farther away, on the terraced slopes, dark forests came to an end. It was warm and we were dreaming of the snow at the port where we had embarked; all of us were on the deck, watching the shores come into view. As we approached, pink flamingos took flight, then settled down again in their places as soon as we had passed by; and their actions made us suspicious of the shores.

We waited; and bitterness filled our gaping hearts.

Will it be here that we shall find a place which will not elude us, or which if it remains does not exert on us a culpable attraction? Or must we, leaning over the deck and watching the shores glide by, move forever onward? *

* *Narcissus* (1891), written to defend the doctrine of Symbolism, depicts Narcissus in the classical pose—bending over the water and viewing not only his own image but the moving panorama of life.

Toward midday we came to a town; it was a sparse settlement stretched out along the seashore. The sea fanned out to form a gulf and, before the town, at low tide, a large coral reef could be seen. Daily fishermen's boats came there to hunt for coral, sponges, and pearl-bearing shells. Since nothing in the town interested us, one of the boats took us toward the coral island. It seemed to rise from the depths of the transparent sea that encircled it; against the background of pale polyps appeared yawning oysters; sponges grew all along the coral reef; green crabs crawled about, and in the fissures, in the shadows, octopuses lay hidden. When the divers came within range, sticky tentacles tried to seize them; but the divers, with wide-open knives, cut off the tentacles, which stuck to their bodies even after they surfaced. The saffron-skinned men were naked, but from their necks hung reticulated sacks for holding shells. They gathered the shells with their great knives, then, their sacks filled, quickly surfaced. When they emerged once more in the open air, their chests shriveled slightly and a fillet of blood which spilled from their mouths and embellished their golden skin almost made them faint.*

We threw new coins into the water; they scintillated as they sank; and when they were about to disappear,

---

* Gide felt a strong attraction, partly sexual and partly intellectual, to the people with whom he had no common intellectual or economic ties, yet was never able to mingle easily with them. His predilection for the moslem culture caused him to travel outside France on various occasions.

the men, leaping from the boat and plunging into the sea, smothered them as one would snuff out a candle. But if it had not been for the joy of looking at the bottom of the sea and seeing the men's blood, these games would not have entertained us; after a while, we came back to the town.

We bathed in excessively warm pools in which children swam and chased each other. Mosaics could be seen on the bottom through the green water, and two symmetrically arranged figures of pink marble spilled perfumes into round basins; the perfumes fell into the water in delicate cascades, with soft sound. Coming up to the statues, we stretched out our hands toward the basins, and the perfumes ran down the length of our arms and trickled over our hips. When we dived back into the water, it seemed to scald us. A scented vapor rose to the translucid ceiling; it condensed and formed droplets that made the light turn blue and from the ceiling these droplets fell one by one into the water.

And since we were overcome by torpor when we breathed in this warm vapor, we remained motionless, suspended, hopelessly entranced in the wondrous green and blue water, with only a soft light spilling over it and the arms of the slender children turning blue in the light as droplets fell from the ceiling and splashed monotonously into the pool.

... At nightfall the sea became phosphorescent; fires along the bank leaped at each other, as did the waves. The night was aflame; the sailors and the spurious men went back to their women, and the thought of their embraces tormented us, for the night was truly too passionate. An enormous blushing moon rose above the waves and cast its reflection over the already luminous sea. Brown boats cut through its furrows on their way back to the shores. Only the sound of waves and flickering fires was heard in the night.

And from the forests vampires came on broad wings and hovered near the bare feet, near the lips of drowsy fishermen, sucked out their lives and lulled them to sleep with the silent beating of their wings.*

Morgain was feverish. He asked us to put eternal snow on his forehead.

We put into port alongside an island dominated by a very high mountain. We went ashore; Nathanael, Ydier, Alain, Axel and I walked toward the snows. For a long time afterwards, we were still thinking of the island, for it was calm and enticing; because of glaciers that had moved all the way down to the valley, the air that circulated was almost cool. We walked along, happy to experience such calm.

On reaching the foot of a translucid glacier, we saw a clear fountain. It flowed softly from beneath the ice; a polished sheet of quartz, which it had hollowed out in the shape of a chalice, served as a receptacle. We filled our crystal vial in order that we might take some of the water back to Morgain.

Cold water of ineffable purity! In the goblets from

* There is much to support the theory that for Gide art was a means of avoiding painful reality. As a child and as a writer he preferred pleasurable fantasies to painful realities.

which we drank, it still retained its sky-color. It was so limpid and so blue that it seemed to have lost none of its depth. It was still as fresh as hiemal water. It was as pure and intoxicating as the early morning air in the mountains. As we drank the water, a seraphic happiness enraptured us; we dipped our hands in it; we dampened our eyelids; it washed away the ravages of fevers, and its subtle virtue penetrated even our thoughts, as lustral water. Afterwards, the countryside seemed to us more beautiful, and we marveled at everything around us.

Toward noon we returned to the sea and walked along the shoreline. From the sand we gathered golden pebbles and rare shells washed ashore by the tide, and on the tamarisks along the beach we found emerald-colored beetles.

Near the sea grew a plant whose flowers were always crowned with butterflies. The butterflies were indistinguishable from the petals, and this made the flowers seem to have wings. We knew that spring butterflies, the first butterflies in May, are white and yellow, like primroses and hawthorns; summer butterflies variegated, like all flowers, and autumn butterflies the color of dead leaves; but these, on pink flowers, had the transparent wings of butterflies from high summits, and the corollas of the flowers were visible through their wings.

As we walked along the shoreline, we came upon a mysterious child who was sitting on the sand, lost in revery. His huge eyes were as blue as a glacial sea;

his skin shimmered like lilies and his hair was like a cloud struck by the sun at dawn.* He was trying to understand some words that he had traced on the sand. He spoke; his voice spilled from his lips like the morning bird shaking off the dew and taking flight; we would gladly have given him our shells, our insects and our pebbles, all that we had, so sweet was his charming voice. He smiled with infinite sadness. We wanted to take him to the ship, but he crouched on the sand and resumed his calm meditation.

We departed. The walk through this island had given us strength, and when the *Orion* again set sail, we gazed upon the open sea ahead of us and felt a tremor in our hearts.

We did not bathe that day.

---

* Gide here added a footnote—the simple word *Novalis*. Friedrich Leopold, Freiherr von Hardenberg (1772-1801), was a pioneer of the Romantic movement. His long unfinished *Heinrich von Ofterdingen,* which relates a hero's quest for the mysterious blue flower is an allegory of the writer's life.

VII

For the seventh time the ship stopped. This island where we disembarked full of hope and from which we were not to depart until long thereafter, was for many the end of the voyage. Those of us who continued onward, leaving behind us so many dead companions and hopes, were never again to see the splendid lights which had previously roused us. But sailing aimlessly under a morose sky, we regretted the town—beautiful in spite of all its sensuality—the royal town, the palaces of Haïatalnefus with their terraces that frightened us when we walked on them because their sheer beauty made them unsafe. Terraces! Merciful Bactrian terraces bathed in morning sunshine! Hanging gardens, gardens with a view of the sea! Palaces no longer seen but still longed for! How we would have loved you if not for this island!

The winds had ceased completely. But wary, because of a certain splendor that made the air along the shores vibrate, only four disembarked at first. From the *Orion* we saw them climb a hillock covered with olives, then return. The island was wide and beautiful, they said; from the hillock one could see plateaus, high smoking mountains and, along the shore that curved inward, the last houses of a town. Since nothing that they had seen justified our first fears, all of us, including the sailors, disembarked and made our way toward the town.

The first inhabitants that we encountered were drawing water beside a fountain; they came up to us as soon as they saw us. They were dressed in sumptuous garments which weighed heavily upon them and fell in straight folds; headdresses in the shape of a diadem gave them a priestly air. They offered their lips to be kissed and their eyes glittered with vicious promises. But when we refused them, these women, whom we had not recognized at first, were horrified; on seeing that we were foreigners, ignorant of the customs of the island, they half-opened their purple cloaks and exposed their pink-painted breasts. When we still rejected them, they were astounded; then, taking our hands, they led us toward the town.

Through the streets roved only admirable creatures. Early in their childhood those not perfectly beautiful, feeling the weight of reprobation, went into seclusion. Not all, however, for some of the most horrible and most deformed ones were pampered and used to satisfy abnormal desires. We saw no men—only boys with the faces of women and women with the faces of boys; sensing the approach of new terrors, they fled toward plateaus inhabited only by men. Since the death of Camaralzaman, the men had all left the town. Maddened by the desire for men, these forsaken women, like those whom we had met, would sometimes venture into the countryside; thinking that some men who had come down from the plateaus might come, they disguised themselves in order to seduce them. We learned this, not at the outset, but only after the queen, having led us into the palace, came to tell us that she was holding us prisoner.

Enticing captivity, more perfidious than harsh jails. These women desired our caresses, and they kept us imprisoned in order that they might satisfy their desires.

From the first day the sailors were lost; then one by one the others fell; but there remained twelve of us who would not give in.

The queen became enamored of us; she had us bathe in warm pools and perfumed us with nitrobenzene; she reclothed us in splendid cloaks; but avoiding her caresses, we thought only of our departure. She thought boredom would overcome our resistance, and long days elapsed. We waited; but over the monotonous Ocean moved not a single gust; the air was as blue as the sea; and we did not know what had become of the ship.

From noon until evening we slept in small rooms with glassed doors that opened out on a wide stairway leading down to the sea. When the rays of the evening sun struck the panes, we would go outside. Then the air was calmer; from the sea there arose a scented coolness; we would inhale the cool air and remain enraptured for a short while before descending; at this hour the sun was plunging into the sea; oblique rays struck the marble steps and infused them with scarlet transparencies. Slowly then, all twelve of us, majestic, symmetrical and solemn because of our sumptuous attire, walked down toward the sun, down to the last step where a light breeze sprayed our robes with foam.

At other times or on other days we would sit, all twelve of us, on a raised throne, each like a king, facing the sea and watching the tide rise and fall; we were hoping that perhaps on the waves would appear a sail or in the sky a cloud swollen by a propitious wind. Restrained by our nobility, we made no gestures and remained silent; but when in the evening our fallen hope departed with the light, then, like a wail of despair, a great sob welled up in our chests. And the queen would come running to gloat over our distress, to study us; but she always found us motionless, our dry eyes gazing toward the place where the sun had set. She saw clearly that we were thinking of the ship, and we dared not ask her what had happened to it.

Since we kept resisting and seemed more austere to her each day, the queen tried to distract us, thinking that in games and festive activities we would forget our voyage and our destinies. They seemed to us very serious and precise; our pride was heightened by this resistance, and underneath the splendor of our cloaks we felt welling in our hearts an irrepressible desire for glorious actions.

Pompous gardens with tiered terraces descended from the palace to the sea. Sea water flowed in through marble canals, and the trees hung low overhead; strong bindweeds interwined, forming swaying bridges and swings. At the mouth of the canals they floated in a dense cluster that resisted the sharpest blades; farther along, the water in the canals was always calm. Boats moved through the canals, and we saw fish swimming in their mysterious shadows; but we dared not bathe there because of stinging crabs and cruel lobsters.

On the shore near the town was a cave to which we were taken by the queen. The boat entered through a narrow opening that vanished from sight soon after we passed through it; the light in traveling through the blue water under the rocks took on the color of the waves whose movements appeared as faint flickers on the walls. The boat followed a circuitous route between two rows of basaltic columns; the air and the diaphanous water intermingled and became indistinguishable; everything was shrouded by bluish light. At the base of the descending columns were sand, algae and rocks from which the indeterminate light seemed to emanate.

Above our heads played the shadow of the boat. In the depths of the cave the sand fanned out into a beach lashed by small waves. We would have liked to swim in this ocean fairyland, but we dared not bathe for fear of crabs and lampreys.

In this manner the queen entertained us; though we continued to resist, our hearts thrilled at the sight of the marvels through which she hoped to seduce us. At night in the boat at sea, watching the stars and constellations wholly unlike those that appear in our skies, we sang:

"Queen! Queen of chimerical islands, queen with necklaces of coral, you whom we would have loved if you had come at dawn, queen of our despair, beautiful Haïatalnefus, oh let us depart!"

Then she said, "Why? What will you do?" and we did not know the answer. She continued:

"Stay with us; I yearn for you. One night, I would have you know, you were sleeping in your rooms; without a sound I came and kissed your eyes, and your soul was refreshed by the kiss that I placed on them. Stay. The winds have fallen, and you no longer have a ship. What will you seek elsewhere?"

And we did not know what to say, for she could not understand that all of this could not satisfy the vast yearning of our souls. We were weeping in our anxiety.

"Madame, oh what should I say to you? Nobility and supreme beauty always draw our tears. As beautiful as you are, Madame, you are not so beautiful as our lives; and the brave deeds that lie before us illuminate our paths like stars."

Then, elated by the night and the ease with which words came, I declaimed, thinking that I could see in the past a reflection of the brave deeds that awaited us:

"Oh! Oh, Madame, if only you knew about the missions and cavalcades of our youth: majestic hunts in the forest; glorious deliverances and the return, in the evening, along the same path and through the dust; and the joy of having accomplished our day's task! And our exhaustion, Madame, and our sad appearance! How serious our lives! And how we bestrode the mountain as the sun sank and shadows claimed the valley; sometimes we felt that we were about to catch our chimeras, and our hearts fluttered with happiness! . . .

The queen kept looking at me, the trace of a smile in her eyes, and asking:

"Is that true?"

But I was so convinced that I said to her:

"Oh, yes, Madame."

As the moon moved onward I cried out:

"I am so sad for her because of her pallor."

Then the queen spoke up:

"What does it matter to you?" she asked. And suddenly the aptness of her question forced me to agree.

And thus the days passed, given over to excursions or festivities.

One evening the queen had playfully dropped a ring from one of her fingers into the deep sea. It was not an expensive ring but had been given to her, like all her rings, by Camaralzaman, her husband. It was old and had an aventurine set in a bezel supported by plaited strands of pale gold. It could still be seen when plants changed their position on the blue sand where pink anemones glistened, pensive and bewildered. Clarion, Agloval and Morgain equipped themselves for diving and descended; I did not follow them—not because I was too bored but because I was too anxious, for the mysterious depths of the sea had always attracted me. They remained underwater for a long time; as soon as they surfaced I questioned them, but they fell into a deep sleep, and when they were awakened they seemed to remember nothing, or to be unwilling to answer me.

"It was so dark all around me that I could see nothing," said Angloval.

"A paralyzing torpor overpowered my thoughts," said Clarion, "and then I could think only of the relucent sleep that one would sleep in this fresh water, lying on the soft algae."

Morgain remained silent and sad, and when I begged him to relate what he had seen, he replied that even if he so willed, he could not find the right words.

Then came new festivities, decorative lights and dances; in this way still other days passed, and we were tormented by the feeling that our superb lives were being wasted on trivial occupations.

We thought of the ship, and we began to evolve a plan of escape. Before the palace stretched the plain, and the open shore curved inward; one could clearly see that the *Orion* was not there on the vast sea. But on the other side of the palace must lie other beaches; the *Orion* must be there. The high walls of the last terraces jutted out into the sea as if to block its approach; secret paths must lead out to it, but only the queen knew where they were. One night when the sea was so low that it withdrew from the base of the walls,

Ydier, Hélain, Nathanael and I set out secretly in search of the ship.

It was still twilight, but there were no longer any sounds. We passed beyond the terraces and found ourselves behind the town; long walls fronted on a small strip of sand onto which gutters spilled their offensive smells. We hastened because of the approaching sea and night, but we thought we might be able to return by another route if the tide should block this one. After the walls came low banks of clay; the space that separated them from the water became narrower and narrower, and the waves finally soaked their base. We stopped, uncertain, to determine what the sea was doing. But the tide was not yet rising; stepping on rocks that jutted out of the water, we continued our search. A promontory came into view; we thought we could see a beach in the distance. Our feet slid over soft plants; gray, crepuscular water, barely distinguishable, splashed feebly between the rocks; uneasiness gripped us, so indeterminate was this water . . . And suddenly the bank came to an end; fear surged through our hearts, for we sensed the ship was there. The night was all embracing. Noiselessly we moved onward a few steps and then, leaning against the last rock, we looked.

The moon was rising over an immense strand; the blue sands shifted, undulated. On the water floated a whole fleet, formidable, vaporous, strange; we dared not proceed. Mysterious shapes passed by; everything seemed to us so fanciful, so uncertain that we fled, gripped by piteous fear; we were guided and bewildered by the moon that rose above the strand and cast our distorted shadows on the rocks and water in front of us.

Our deliverance came about in a most tragic manner. Appearing and spreading throughout the town, but mildly at first, was the horrible and lamentable plague that later ravaged the island, leaving it as forlorn as an immense desert. It was already interfering with the festivities.

... In the morning the fresh juices that we drank on the terraces, the fruits, and the glasses of cold water after walks in the sunshine; and in the evening, worn out by the excitement of the long day, iced lemonade under the trees in the perfumed gardens that led down to the sea; everything—excessively warm baths and idle musings in the presence of the insidious garments of the women—would soon have induced languor, the first symptom of the plague, if the fear of excessive suffering had not prejudiced us against so many pleasures. We resisted smiles, nocturnal entreaties, the desire for satisfying fruits, shadows in the gardens, music; we even stopped singing for fear of growing faint; but in the morning before sunrise we would walk down the beach, immerse our naked bodies in the wholesome water, and draw new strength and comfort from the sea and the air.

Filth deposited in hidden sewers and wash-houses by slovenly townspeople sent up a pestilential exhalation in the evening; and these paludal vapors carried deadly germs. The sailors and the women felt them in their flesh; it was a nascent uneasiness; they used balms to rinse out their mouths and the heavy scent of aromatic oils blended with their hot breath.

That evening even their dances were subdued. Never had the winds been milder; the waves sang and each soul was enchanted by its body. All of their bodies, as beautiful as marble statues, glistened in the shadows; they sought out each other for embraces, but their desire was not sated; their fever was intensified by their embraces; each added the other's ardor to his own. Their kisses were bites; wherever their hands touched, they bled.

All night long they depleted themselves through their false embraces, but morning bathed them in a new dawn; then they went toward the fountains to cleanse their tainted tunics. There, new festivities began; light-headed, they laughed from weariness, and their bursts of laughter echoed through their empty heads. The water from the bath-house had been defiled. They rammed their big poles deep into the slime; clouds of mud arose; bubbles arose and burst; leaning over the edges, they breathed in the pestilential smells, but without alarm; they laughed because they were already sick. They again put on their damp tunics and, chilled, drew comfort from the illusion that their bodies had been revitalized. But in the evening their fever underwent a radical change; they ceased laughing; they were overcome by torpor, and each of them flung himself on the grass-covered lawn and thought only of himself. . . .

On the island were flowers whose bruised corollas discharged a scent like that from a glacial mint. From these plants that grew in the sands they gathered flowering branches, and the petals which they masticated all day long were delightfully refreshing to their dry eyes when placed on their hot eyelids. A soothing sensation permeated their cheeks, penetrated their brains and prompted torpid dreams. They dozed like fakirs. As soon as they ceased their chewing, soothing changed to burning, as happens in the case of sweet-smelling spices or herbs with a peppery flavor. Thirsty, they drank from metal goblets water tinged with tart gooseberry juice. They stopped chewing only to drink.

When their tunics parted and exposed their chests, under their arms, near their breasts, could be seen a purplish bruised spot where the malady had its seat; sometimes their bodies were completely covered with violet drops of sweat. All twelve of us remained silent, too solemn even to cry, and watched our companions die.

Oh! the terrible part was the arrival of the men; they all came down from the plateaus hoping to find women emboldened by desire whom they could infect with the sickness. They came running, hideous, livid; but when they saw that the women were so pale and understood why, they were terrified and ran through the town shouting. Some women still desired them; and as the certainty of death restored in them a sinister boldness, the men and women embraced furiously. They sucked in all the joy they could with a thirst, a mania, a sort of frenzy that struck us dumb with terror; it seemed that they were trying in this way to eliminate the time of remorse. And other women sobbed because they had arrived too late.*

A light wind arose, forced the heavy smoke from the volcanoes back toward the town, and drenched them with gray ashes. Exhausted, they had parted to vomit. Now they were rolling confusedly on the grass, and their entrails were making hideous attempts to come out. So they died, crumpled, twisted, hideous, already decomposed; and silence fell upon the town.

Then clouds appeared; a cold rain toward morning finished glazing their souls and covered them with a muddy shroud formed by water and the ashes.

And we thought of great sails, of departure; but having hoped in vain for so long and under such monotonous circumstances, now that nothing prevented us from departing, we felt so tired, so upset, so concerned over the solemnity of our tasks, so exhausted by everything, that for twelve more days we remained on the big island, sitting on the beach and facing the sea, speechless, pensive, aware of the uncertainty and superfluity of our whims.

And what really made us depart was the unbearable stench of the corpses.

* From his Journals we learn that Gide had periods of happy productivity but seemed during periods of demoralization to draw comfort from the recording of sad events.

SARGASSO SEA

Sargasso Sea; tearful dawn and cheerless flashed on the gray water. Certainly, if I had been able to choose, I would not have rowed toward those latitudes. Boredom! Why say it? One who has not known it will not understand it: one who has known it asks not to be reminded of it. Boredom! Dismal contemplations of the soul, when forbidden splendors and illuminations depart, you claim us. Scintillations have ceased, temptations flee; nothing concerns us now, except ourselves, our disenchanted dawns.

The ashes of twilight fall on faded suns, and the mists of boredom on great surgings of desire.

Psychology! Psychology! Science of the soul and all its vanity, which the soul attributes to you! Ashen fruits which we might have consumed; desires that might have stained our gums. Oh, temptations which we once deplored and dreaded. Desires! At least when we resisted you, our souls were not idle; we did not yield; we hoped that temptations would go away, and now that they have, boredom spreads endlessly across the gray sea!

Gelatinous fucuses uncoil on the thick sea. Infinitely long strands of algae float on the surface and stretch sinuously toward the horizon; we thought at first on seeing them at dawn that they were reptiles but they were not; there was nothing in the distance except these long, docile algae.

We looked at the compass, and our waning faith allowed our bleak knowledge to increase. On charting our latitude, we saw that we had reached that point which sailors call "The Trap" because the oleaginous sea is so calm.

The sea in spots was a mass of algae, and soon we were sailing between two long lines of sargassum; far apart and loose at first, they began to coagulate; gradually they drew together, and in the ever narrowing channel of free water that separated them, the *Orion* became a felucca. Soon the long spirals of fucuses gave way to thick tangles of soft leaves and a viscous, vegetable substance, barely penetrable, soon seemed to swell and rose slightly above the water in shallow places, where it formed low, slimy mountains. The channel undulated between their curves.

On the third day appeared the first fluvial plants; the felucca was moving slowly up a placid tributary.

On the fourth day smoke-colored herons hunted for worms in the mud on the shores; behind them lay a level sward. At night clouds caught in the pale light of the dying day were reflected in the river which, because of the shadows that obscured its banks, seemed to flow in a straight line; the oars became tangled in the reeds alongside the felucca as it went around the bends.

On the seventh day we met my dear Ellis who was waiting for us under an apple tree on the sward. She had been there for fourteen days, having arrived by land sooner than we; she wore a polka dot dress and carried a cherry-colored parasol; beside her was a vanity case containing toilet articles and a few books; on her arm was a Scottish shawl; she was eating an escarole salad and reading *Prolegomena to Any Future Metaphysic*.* We had her climb into the boat.

Our reunion was rather dull, and since we were accustomed to discussing only what we both knew about and had followed different routes, we found nothing to say. For three days we watched the steep banks in silence; then the new terrains that we had passed through provided us with another opportunity to exchange comments.

The sky was pale, the countryside discolored. Along the glaucous banks lined with green plants and ashes were placid storks which had returned from their quests. Ellis thought that their feet were disproportionate; that is how I found out about her disturbing

* The grotesque figure of Ellis recalls Gide's inability to fuse in a normal manner the physical and the spiritual. Ellis appears in his Journals as Em, and elsewhere as Alissa, Emmanuèle or Madeleine. "All purity, love, and tenderness" in his other works, she is really his cousin (later his wife) Madeleine Rondeaux.

superficiality; but I said nothing to her about her cherry-colored umbrella in the tearful setting, reserving the question of imperfections for subsequent conversations.

The uninspiring, verdigris-encrusted banks between which we were still rowing, so flat, so calm, so confining, so consistently the same, offered nothing to tempt us to stop our monotonous escapade at one point rather than another. The sole episode in our rash adventure was the boat on the calm stream, imprisoned between the banks, and since it kept moving along with us, we remained in it simply because we did not know where to disembark. And when one evening we finally did set foot on an indifferent bank, it was rather because of the hour, because of the approach of twilight.

A tattered mist hovered over the bleak water and clung to the reeds along the banks. We decided to spend the night on the sward; Ellis had to stay in the boat; she wrapped herself in her shawl because of the humidity, placed her vanity case under her head, and fell asleep among the reeds bruised by the anchored boat.

After a dreamless night came a cheerless awakening; there was no red in the sky, which was brightened only in the morning by a sad and chilling dawn. The light was so faint that we were still expecting the dawn when we glimpsed the sun, which had already risen, behind a cloud. We rejoined Ellis; she was sitting in the felucca, reading the *Theodicy*. Irritated I took the book from her; the others remained silent; there was a painful moment of consternation; and since our course was unsure and our destinies were no longer linked by a common goal, our wills diverged and each of us made his own way inland.

I did not have the heart to go far; only toward a little grove of beech trees. But I did not even reach the grove and threw myself instead into the shadow of the first shub; since I was no longer in view of the others, and since I felt my strength ebbing away and the past returning, I put my head in my hands and cried wretchedly.

Evening fell on the pimpernel-spotted prairie; then I said a little prayer, stood up and returned to the abandoned boat.

Ellis in the boat was reading the *Treatise on Contingency;* exasperated, I wrenched the book from her hands, threw it into the river.

"Don't you know, wretched Ellis," I shouted, "that books are temptation? And our goal was glorious actions. . . ."

"Glorious?" said Ellis, looking at the uninspiring plain.

"Oh! I know that it doesn't seem that way; I know everything that you can say. Silence! Silence!" On the verge of tears, I hid my face from her and stared at the water in the stream.

My companions returned one by one, and when all of us had reassembled in the boat, each felt so acutely the desire of all that no one dared ask whether the others had seen nothing; instead, propriety caused each to make a vain statement to disguise the inanity of his vision:

"I saw, I saw," said Aguisel, "rows of dwarf birches on a clay knoll."

"As for me," said Eric, "on a sandy plain I saw grasshoppers feeding on bitter grass."

"And you, Urien?" said Axel.

"A pimpernel-spotted field."

"Morgain?"

"Forests of blue pines near the seashore."

"Ydier?"

"Some abandoned quarries. . . ."

And since the hour was late and we had lost interest in the discussion, we fell asleep.

The next day I awoke late; all the others had already risen, and I saw them sitting on the shore. They were all reading. Ellis had passed out some brochures on ethics. I grabbed her vanity case; in it were three memorandum-books, *The Life of Franklin*, a little treatise on temperate climates, and Desjardins' *Present Duty*. Even as I searched the vanity case, I was preparing an apostrophe; when everything was ready, I threw down the case. It sank in the river. Two huge tears ran down Ellis' cheeks. Not because I was moved but because I sensed our common misery, my irritation suddenly vanished and censure gave way to compassion.

"We are indeed miserable," I cried out. "So far our voyage has been a failure. What does our cheerless plain mean at this moment in our history? Or what is the significance of our being on the plain? Any suspicion of futility will torment our hearts and allow their virtue to be diffused. Lord! In the face of futility, we shall no longer have either faith or courage. Now we are going to weaken—or must we embrace piety? We have cherished our pride, and our nobility has suffered from the asperity of our victories. Our virtue derives solely from resistance; but around us now everything gives way, everything crumbles, and we are no longer aware of our courage. Our tranquil past resurges in us like a regret. Majestic and profound night of wild ecstasy! Texts of truth where often there flickered a metaphysical flame! Algebras and theodicies, studies! We had left you for something else. Oh, for something else indeed! We set out one morning because we had learned through study that we must manifest our essence; we went off into the world in search of revealing actions, knowing nothing of the tenebrous valley that connected the lofty room where we dreamed to the world where men lived—the valley so terrible and so mysterious that I expected death there, so tenebrous that my eyes mistook the waves for lights when finally I stood before the long-sought sea. Afterwards we saw beaches, profuse vegetation, gardens traversed by warm streams, palaces, imposing terraces whose memory causes despair; we saw every smile, heard every plea, and still we resisted; not even Queen Haïatalnefus, deceitful and perfumed, could overcome our resistance. We were preserving ourselves for something else. Through a calculated—indeed, I ought to say esthetic—progression, our courage and desire grew with our resistance; and we were anticipating a climactic event. Now our boat is going to founder in the mire. Oh! Ours is truly a history of failure, abject failure. What can happen next? Nothing matters to us, such is the pall cast on the future by our boredom; our noble souls will succumb to disinterest in their task. No matter what happens, it will always be unimportant. Logical sequences are broken; we have left the salutary paths. Let us remember the detached islands; they floated like abandoned ships, no longer linked to the world. That is the saddest thing that can happen. One can not start all over when futility lies ahead. We are completely lost. We are more miserable by far than my inept words can suggest to you; more miserable by far than we are aware, for the apathy that engulfs us is beginning to dull our souls. I have spoken too long and said too much. Disordered things require incoherent statements; I shall conclude with a few alliterations." Letting my voice fall suddenly until it was only a murmur, I whispered this cadence:

". . . The grasshopper of the sands will sing."

All those sitting on the bank had heard me out; but my peroration seemed to them incongruous and they shook with undissimulated laughter; I had hoped that it would awaken us from our torpor.* Ellis had understood nothing; I felt suddenly irritated but showed no

---

* We learn from his Journals that Gide frequently suffered embarrassment over his inability to say the right words at the right time.

sign of it. She opened wide her inquisitive eyes; she was waiting for me to continue.

"I have finished, dear Ellis," I said. "Let's walk through the grass. You are sweet and delightful today. The air will be good for you." **

I think it would be wearisome to recount our stroll; I prefer to speak of a cave which we entered but could not explore to any great extent because it was partially filled with stagnant water; we could nevertheless see high vaults shrouded in darkness; galleries that seemed endless; places where the walls of the caverns arched to form a ceiling, lethargic bats hung like fruit. I plucked one for Ellis, who had not yet seen any of them. The best part about the cave was that, after we left its oppressive gloom, the light outside seemed somewhat less sad. It was in the cave that Ellis contracted marsh-fever and I first had terrifying doubts about her identity.

While the others were getting back into the boat that evening, Ydier, Nathanaël and I, feeling vaguely once more a desire to live, started inland. Then we had a strange adventure whose mysteriousness still torments us, for it was unique and unrelated to anything else that occurred during our voyage.

Night had fallen; the wind swept across the rushes in the moors; fires hovered over the peat-bogs; afraid of the quagmires, we walked slowly. A tinkling sound

** Up to this point the narrator has used the familiar pronoun *tu* in addressing Ellis. Here he uses the polite form *vous*.

broke the silence and caused us to stop, surprised. Like a vaporous form, a white woman emerged, floated ethereally, rose above the marsh; she shook a chalice-like bell which she held in her hand. Our first impulse was to flee; then, somewhat reassured by her ethere-ality, we were about to call out to her when she began to disintegrate into shapeless mist, either higher or more distant, and the tinkling sound began to fade away; but it lingered still, and we were beginning to think that fatigue had made us the victims of some illusion when, walking onward, we heard it nearer, again clear, skimming the ground, at times uncertain, alternately blatant and hesitant, then plaintive, imploring; bending down in the darkness for a better view, we found a poor lamb lost on the moor, bewildered, its wool dampened by the dark. Around its neck was the little bell. We lifted up the lamb that had gone astray and removed its bell.

But once again a noise broke the stillness and slowly there emerged from the slough a woman who wore a veil resembling a mortuary shroud, her gray veil clung like mist to the rush-bed. The drooping lily inclined its chalice earthward; its sounds spilled out like seeds. And, as she fled, I saw her stoop down near a recess in the darkness and hang her lily like a bell from the neck of a waiting lamb. We found the lamb on the plain.

A third form appeared; sweat covered her face; behind her floated her train, like a tattered cloth, over the leaves of the rushes. And I saw her hold out the lily as she disintegrated and leave the disconsolate lamb with the bell which her dissolving hand had tied to its wool.

In the same way twelve women appeared; we found the lambs afterwards and, like shepherds without crooks, used our hands to guide the flock through the night along unknown paths, between clumps of rushes and off-shoots of ranunculuses.

When we returned to the boat, dawn was beginning to glow. Ellis was in some pain and slightly delirious. I noticed that day, for the first time I think, that her hair was completely blond; blond, nothing more.

The felucca began once more to move up the fluvial waters; long days passed in this way, but they were too monotonous to relate. The banks were always so alike that we seemed not to be making any headway. The stream slowed imperceptibly, stopped, and we rowed through stagnant water, deep and dark. On each bank stood a row of cypresses; from each branch there fell a somber shadow that weighed heavily on our souls. We heard our oars fall into the stream with a muffled rhythm, then the water lifted up by the oars fall back like heavy tears; we heard nothing else. Leaning over the water, each saw his face enlarged and enveloped by darkness for, because of the cypresses which had become gigantic, the water no longer reflected the sky. We looked often at the black water and often at our faces in the water. Ellis babbled incoherently in the bottom of the boat and uttered prophecies. We understand that we had come to the climactic point of our history. And soon, in fact, the gigantic cypresses grew smaller. But we were too overcome by silence and by darkness to be very astounded by a disconcerting phenomenon: the water was beginning to flow, but to flow in the opposite direction. Now we were going back down the mysterious stream. And as in a story read backwards, or as in a flashback, we were retracing our voyage; we came back to the familiar steep banks and again lived through all our boredom. The stolid storks were again fishing for mudworms . . . I shall not relate the monotonous scene again; it was too trying to relate the first time. I shall not bewail the lack of proportions in the history; however for if it took as long to retrace the lethargic stream as to ascend it the first time, I was not aware of this fact; I no longer watched the cheerless banks and dour water glide by; only the thought of Ellis made me oblivious to the passage of the hours; or, leaning over the reflection of my unknown self in the water, I sought in my sad eyes to gain a better understanding of my thoughts, and I read in my tight lips the bitterness of regret that tightens them. Ellis! do not read these lines! I am not writing them for you! You would never understand the despair that grips my soul.

But the stream of boredom came to an end; the waters again became clearer; the low banks disappeared, and again we were at sea. Ellis was slightly delirious in the enlarged boat. The seawater gradually became so limpid that we could see the rocks on the bottom. Reflecting on all the boredom of the previous day, on the perfumed baths of the past, I studied the underwater plain; I recalled that Morgain, in the gardens of Haïatalnefus, had gone beneath the waves and walked in the algae. I was about to speak when I glimpsed among the algae on the sand, like an ethereal vision, a sunken city. Still uncertain, I kept looking, not daring to utter a word; the boat was advancing slowly. The walls of the city were visible; sand had filled most of the streets; some, however, still looked green like deep valleys between the raised walls. The whole town was green and blue. Algae reached from balconies down to the fucus-lined squares. One could see the shadow of the church. The shadow of the boat glided over the tombs of the cemetery; green mosses slept on, undisturbed. The sea was silent; fish played in the waves.

"Morgain! Morgain! Look!" I shouted.

He was already looking.

"Will you be sorry?" he inquired. As was my custom, I did not reply; but giving way suddenly to a burst of lyricism occasioned by the boredom we had experienced and the joy of seeing once more a town, a silent town, I exclaimed:

"We should be, oh! so comfortable under the cool water on the porch of the sunken church! The taste of the shadows and the humidity. The sound of bells under the waves. And the calm, Morgain! . . . Morgain, you can not know what torments me. She was waiting, but I was mistaken; Ellis is not like that. No Ellis is not a blond; I was sadly mistaken; I remember now that her hair was black and that her eyes sparkled as bright as her soul. Her soul was vivacious and violent, and yet her voice was very calm for she was contemplative. And the waif that I found on the bank was frail and forlorn. Why? First her parasol displeased me; then her shawl; then all her books irritated me. Yet one does not travel to recover one's old thoughts; and then she cried when I brought these things to her attention. First I said to myself: 'Oh! How she has changed!' but I see clearly now that she is not the same person. And this is still the most absurd episode of the voyage. As soon as I saw her on the bank, I felt that she was misplaced. But what shall I do now? This is all very distracting, Morgain, and I dislike sentimental states of dejection."

But Morgain seemed not to understand; then I started over in a milder manner. . . .

It was on the same day, a little after this serious conversation, that thin sheets of ice first appeared on the horizon. A current was carrying them toward temperate waters; they came from frozen seas. They were not melting, I suppose, but dissolving into the blue air, imperceptibly more fluid; They subtilized like fog. And the first sheets encountered, because the water was still almost warm, had become so thin, so diaphanous and diluted that the boat had moved along without our noticing them until alerted by the sudden coolness.

Toward evening their numbers kept increasing, as

did their size. We moved through them; as they became even more dense, the boat would strike them and scarcely cut through them. Night fell, and we would have lost sight of them completely had not the light from the stars shone through them pale, purified and magnified. Thus through an imperceptible transition that defies narration, after the splendid shores and sunlit gardens, we were finally to pass through a morose climate and frozen seas and come to arid polar shores.

And imperceptibly also, languishing from her sickness, each day Ellis grew paler, giddier and more blond; she was becoming less and less real, and seemed to be fading away.

"Ellis," I said to her finally, by way of preparing her for what was to come, "you are an obstacle to my union with God, and I can love you only if you too are fused in God himself." *

And when the felucca reached a boreal region where wisps of smoke rose from the huts of the Eskimos, when we left her on the shore and immediately set sail for the Pole, she had already lost almost every vestige of reality.

And we also left there Yvon, Hélain, Aguisel and Lambègue—who were sick with boredom and seemed about to die from drowsiness—and sailed calmly on toward the Pole.

* Urien continues to use the polite form *vous* in addressing Ellis. Gide revealed the ambivalent nature of his love for Madeleine, and her patient suffering because of it, in *Et nunc manet in te,* written in 1947 and issued publicly in 1951.

VOYAGE TO A FROZEN SEA

A rather dilatory auroral sky; purple flashes on the sea where pale blue sheets of ice became iridescent. A rather chilling awakening because the limpid air was no longer pursued by warm breezes. The boreal region where we had left wan Ellis and our four sick companions the day before, though still visible in the distance, was on the verge of disappearing; a delicate buoy far out on the horizon linked the sky to the last waves and seemed to lift and lull the vanishing land. All eight of us assembled on the deck for a morning prayer, serious but not sad; then we raised our solemn voices and felt once more the tide of seraphic joy that had surged through us on the day when we drank crystalline spring water. Then aware of our joyous wills and wishing to seize them and sense them rather than to allow them to vanish, I said to them:

"The hard trials are over. Far from us now are the morose banks where we thought we would die of boredom, farther still the shores with their forbidden pleasures; let us acknowledge that we are happy to have known them. For one can reach this point only through them; the loftiest cities are reached by the most perilous routes; we are going toward the divine city. Yesterday's tarnished sun is tinged with rose. Resistance first quickened our wills; nor was our idleness on the gray swards futile, for when the landscape disappeared, we were left with our wills completely free; because of our boredom, our indeterminate souls managed in those regions to become sincere. And when we act, now, it will surely be in keeping with our aims." *

The sun was rising as we began our prayers; the sea radiated with reflected splendors; rays shot across the waves, and the illuminated sheets of ice, vibrant and responsive, shuddered.

Toward midday some whales appeared; they were swimming in a flock; they would dive under the sheets of ice and reappear farther away; but they stayed at a distance from the ship.

It was now necessary to steer clear of mountains of ice; as their bases were slowly melted away by waters still not very cold, they would suddenly capsize; their prismatic peaks crumbled and disappeared in the agitated sea, churned the water like a tempest, shot up

* Gide never tired of stressing the Biblical precept that self-affirmation is accomplished through self-negation. Not surprisingly, his deep-seated religious bent was counterbalanced by an extraordinary imaginative sexuality. Tortured by desire, he would pray for release from the temptation of the flesh only to recant and beg to remain carnal and lustful until death.

again with cascades all around them, and kept oscillating for a long time in the tumultuous waters, uncertain of their posture. The majestic impact of their fall echoed across the sonorous waves. Sometimes walls of ice fell into the spouts of foam, and all these moving mountains were incessantly transformed.

Toward evening we saw one so large that it was no longer transparent; at first we mistook it for a new territory covered with immense glaciers. Rivulets plummeted from its summits; white bears ran along its edges. The ship came so close to it that its main yard brushed against a snag and shattered some delicate icicles.

We saw some in which were imbedded huge stones torn from the natal glacier and which therefore carried over the waves fragments of alien rock.

We saw others which had imprisoned whales when drawn together by some mysterious force; above the level of the ocean, they seemed to be swimming in the air. Leaning over the bridge, we watched the moving icebergs.

Evening fell. At sunset the mountains were opalescent. New ones appeared; they trailed laminated algae, which, long and fine as hair, appeared first as captive sirens, then as a vast reticulation; the moon shone through as a jellyfish in a net, as nacreous holothurian; then moving freely through the open sky, the moon turned azure-colored. Pensive stars went astray, whirled, plunged into the sea.

Toward midnight appeared a gigantic vessel; the

moon illuminated it mysteriously; its rigging stood motionless; the bridge was dark. It passed close beside us; there was no sound of oars, no noise from the crew. We finally realized that it was caught in the ice, between two icebergs that had closed in on it. It passed on by, silently, and disappeared.

Toward morning, a little while before dawn, a cool breeze brought alongside us an islet of purest ice; in the middle, like a globed fruit, like a magic egg, gleamed an immortal jewel. It was a morning star on the waves, and we could not tire of gazing at it. It was as pure as a ray from Lyra; it vibrated at dawn like a melody; but as soon as the sun rose, the ice that had encased it melted and allowed it to fall into the sea.

That day we fished for whales.

This marks the end of my memories and the beginning of my undated journal.

❋   ❋   ❋

Into the abyss transplendent with tempest-tossed spume, where no man had ever intruded upon the savage feasts of the albatrosses and eiders, Eric descended, swinging like a diver from a thick elastic cord and brandishing at the end of his naked arm a wide swan-slaying knife. A humid current rises from the depths where the green waves writhe and the wind drives the spume. The great frightened birds wheel and deafen him with the beating of their wings. Bending over and gripping the rock to which the cord is attached, we watch: Eric is above their nests; he descends into the heart of the turmoil; in snow-colored feathers and exquisite down sleep the young eiders; Eric the bird-killer puts his hand on the covey; terrified, the little ones awaken and struggle, trying to escape; but Eric buries the knife in their feathers and laughs when he feels their warm blood on his hands. The blood streams down their feathers, and their beating wings splatter it on the rock. Their blood streams down to the water, and their blood-drenched down is scattered by the waves. The great startled birds are trying to protect their young! Eric, menaced by their claws, slashes them with his knife. And then from the waves arises a vortex of enraged spume; driven between the walls of the abyss by the sea wind, white as the swans' down, it rises, rises, rises, and driven furiously upward with its neverending spirals of feathers, disappears in the sky which we see, whirlpool blue, when we look upward.

On these schistous cliffs the guillemots build their nests. The females remain perched; the males fly around them; they cry out stridently and their cries and the noise of their wings deafen anyone who approaches. They fly in such great hordes that they darken the sky in passing; they wheel ceaselessly. Grave, motionless, never shrieking, the females stand expectantly in a row on a huge ridge where the rock overhangs slightly. They sit on their solitary eggs, deposited there furtively, like droppings, and not in nests but on the bare sloping rock. They sit there, rigid and grave, holding the eggs between their feet and tails to keep them from rolling off.

The ship ventured between the sheer cliffs, into a dark, narrow fiord; the rocks seemed to drop sharply to unknown depths in the transparent water, appearing at times to be the reflection of the cliffs; but the depths were dark and the cliffs white with birds. The males above our heads made so much noise that we could not hear each other. We were advancing slowly; they seemed not to see us. But after Eric, a skilled slinger, hurled a few stones into the opaque cloud and killed several of them with each stone, causing them to fall near the ship, then their redoubled cries enraged their mates on the cliff; leaving behind the nuptial rock and the hope of progeny, all of them took flight, emitting horribly strident screams. It was a fearsome army; we were ashamed of the commotion, especially when we saw all the doomed eggs, now forsaken and no longer held against the ridge, roll down the cliff. They rolled the entire length of the cliff, their broken shells leaving horrible white and yellow trails. Some of the more devoted brooders tried in taking flight to carry their eggs in their claws, but the eggs soon fell out and broke on the blue sea, dirtying the water. We were upset by the commotion and left in great haste, for the terrible stench of the coveys was beginning to engulf us.

. . . In the evening, at the time for prayers, Paride

had not returned; we looked for him and called out to him until night, but we were unable to find out what had happened to him.

The Eskimos live in snow huts; their huts, stretched out across the plain, look like tombstones; but their souls are entombed with their bodies; a wisp of smoke rises from each hut. The Eskimos are ugly; they are small; there is no tenderness in their love-making; they are not voluptuous and their joy is theological; they are neither evil nor good; their cruelty is unmotivated. Inside their huts it is dark; one can hardly breathe there. They neither work nor read; nor do they slumber; a small lighted lamp mitigates the long night; as the night is motionless, they have never known the meaning of an hour; as they need not hurry, their thoughts are slow; induction is unknown to them, but from three tenuous hypotheses they deduct a metaphysics; and the succession of their thoughts, interrupted from start to finish, devolves from God to man, while their life becomes this succession; they measure their age by the point which they have reached; some have never managed to arrive at the point of their existence; others have passed it by; still others have not noticed it. They have no common tongue; they are forever reckoning. Oh! I could say much more, for I understand them quite well. They are stunted, pugnosed, slovenly. Their women have no diseases; they make love in the dark.

I am speaking of the more intelligent Eskimos; there

are others who, at the dawning of the solemn day, cut short the succession of the syllogism and depart for the frozen sea and the melting snow in search of reindeer and moose. They also fish for whales and return with the dark, laden with a new supply of blubber.

Each climate has its rigors, each land its diseases. In the warm lands we had seen the plague; near the marshlands, lingering illnesses. Now an illness was springing up from the very absence of sensual delights. The salty provisions, the lack of fresh fruits and vegetables, and the studied resistance in which we took such great pride; the joy of living wretchedly in unkind lands, and the strong attraction of the outside world on our enraptured souls gradually eroded our strength; and while our souls had then longed, serene, to undertake supreme conquests, scurvy was beginning to afflict all of us and we remained dejected on the deck of the ship, trembling for fear that we would die before finishing our tasks.* Oh, chosen tasks! Most precious tasks! For four days we remained in that condition, not far from the land of our expectation; we saw its icy peaks plunging into the slushy sea; and I believe that our voyage would indeed have come to an end at that point if not for the exquisite liquor that Eric had taken from the Eskimos' hut.

Our blood had become too thin; it was escaping from all over our bodies; it oozed from our gums, from our nostrils, from our eyelids, from under our nails; it

* In 1890 Gide had written of his intense suffering because everyone did not already know "what later I hope to be."

seemed at times to be nothing more than a stagnant humor and almost to cease circulating; the slightest movement made it pour out as from a tilted cup; under the skin, in the tenderest areas it formed livid spots; our heads swam and we were overcome by a feeling of nausea; our necks ached; because our teeth were loose and shook in their alveoli, we could not eat dry sea biscuit; cooked in water it formed a thick pap in which our teeth stuck and remained. Rice tore the skin from our gums; about all we could do was drink. And lying listlessly on the deck all day long, we dreamed of ripe fruits, with fresh tasty meat, of fruits from the islands we had once known, from the pernicious islands. But even then I believe that we would have refused to taste them. We rejoiced because Paride was no longer with us and did not share our suffering. But the hemostatic liquor cured our sickness.

It was the evening of the last day; the sun that marked the season's end had disappeared on the horizon; a crepuscular glow remained long after its disappearance. The sunset was without agony, without purple on the clouds; the sun had disappeared slowly; its refracted rays still reached us. But it was already beginning to become very cold; the sea around us had frozen once more, imprisoning the ship. The ice thickened by the hour and constantly threatened to crush the ship; it offered us only the flimsiest protection, and we resolved to leave it. But I want to state clearly that our decision resulted neither from despair nor from timorous prudence but rather from a maniacal urge, for we could still break the ice, flee from the winter and follow the course of the sun; but that would have taken us backward. And so, preferring the harshest shores, provided that they were new, we moved toward the night, our day having come to an end. We knew that happiness is not simply escape from sadness; we were going, proud and strong, beyond the worst sorrows to the purest joy.

From parts of the ship we had fashioned a sled. After hitching the big reindeer to the sled, we began to load it with wood, axes and ropes. The last rays were disappearing as we set out toward the pole. On the deck of the ship was one spot, hidden by piles of cordage, which we never went near. Oh sad day's end, when before leaving the ship, I walked the full length of the deck! Behind the rolls of cordage, when I untied them to take them along, alas, what did I see?

Paride!

We had sought for him in vain; I supposed that he, too weak to stir and too sick to reply, had hidden there like a dog searching for a place to die. But was this really Paride?

He was hairless, beardless; his teeth lay white on the deck around him, where he had spat them out. His skin was mottled, like a piece of cloth on which the colors have run; it was violet and pearl; nothing was more pitiful to see. He had lost his eyelashes, and at first I was unable to determine whether he was looking at us or at something else, for he could no longer smile. His huge, swollen, mummified, spongy gums had retracted and split his lips and now bulged outward like a large fruit; protruding from the middle was one white tooth, his last. He tried to extend his hand; his bones were too fragile and broke. I wanted to grasp his hand; it fell apart in mine, leaving between my fingers blood and rotted flesh. I think that he saw tears in my eyes, for he seemed to understand then that it was he who was crying, and I think that he still nurtured some hope concerning his condition which my tears of pity dissipated, for suddenly he uttered a raucous cry which was supposed to be a sob, and with the hand that I had not crushed, in a gesture of despair, a tragic and truly hopeless gesture, seizing the tooth and his lips, ironically and as if in jest, he suddenly tore out a great strip of flesh and fell back, dead.

That evening, as a sign of mourning and farewell, we burned the ship. Night was approaching majestically, moving in slowly. The flames leapt up triumphantly; the sea was aflame; the great masts and beams burned and then, the vessel having been consumed, the purple flames sank once again. Leaving the irreparable past, we set out for the polar sea.

Silence of night on the snow. Nocturnal silence. Solitude, and you, calm relief of death. Vast timeless plain; the sun's last rays have withdrawn. All shapes are frozen; cold holds sway on the calm plain, and stillness—and stillness. And serenity. O pure rapture of our souls! Nothing stirs in the air, but a congealed radiance emanates from the glistening icebergs and hovers in the air. All is pale nocturnal blue—shall I say lunar blue?

The moon. Alone in these ecstatic surroundings, I prayed. "Ellis! Ellis! you* who are not the one whom I have found; sweet Ellis, is it here that you have been waiting for me? I would go still farther, but I am waiting for you to speak—and all will soon be over."

I sought her lost figure—and my soul spoke its prayer. Then the night reclaimed its silence, and all its serenity.

Then why await the dawn? No one knows when it will come. There is no time for waiting. After sleeping for a little while, we set out by night for the pole.

Deposits of pure gypsum! Salt quarries! Tombstone-white marble! Mica! All is whiteness in the dark. Light hoarfrosts, smiling by day and flashing like gems by night! Snowdrifts! Congealed avalanches! Dunes of moondust, eider feathers on sea foam, icecaps with taciturn hopes!

The hours glided by as we walked slowly through the snow; our grave, unhurried gestures emphasized the solemnity of our undertaking. Thus all seven of us —Alain, Axel, Morgain, Nathanaël, Ydier, Eric and I —moved toward our tasks.

Eric and the others were sleeping; the hut was calm; outside, a starless night on the vast rimy plain; above the plain, because of its whiteness, the night had

* The familiar form *tu* is used here and in the following pages by both Urien and Ellis.

grown somewhat pale; a faint gleam rimmed the earth; I sought a place to pray. As I was kneeling and beginning my prayer, I saw Ellis. She was sitting on a rock nearby, pensive; her dress was snow-covered, her hair blacker than the night.

"Ellis! So it is you," I sobbed. "Oh, I knew it was you!"

But she remained silent, and I said to her:

"Do you know what sad experiences I have lived through since I lost you? What desolate regions I have crossed since your hand ceased to guide me? One day, on the bank of a stream, I thought I had again found you, but it was only a woman. Oh, forgive me! I have longed for you for so long. Where will you lead me now through this night near the pole, Ellis, my sister?"

"Come," she said to me. And taking me by the hand, she led me to the top of a tall rock from which the sea was visible. I looked, and suddenly the night was torn asunder as a vast aurora borealis spread out over the waves. It was reflected in the sea; there was a silent trickling of phosphorus, a calm precipitation of flashes; and the silence of these astounding splendors was like the voice of God.* It seemed that the purple and pink flames, incessantly agitated, were a palpitation of the Divine Will. All was silent; my dazzled eyes closed;

* The metaphor of phosphorus and its glow, as indivisible as body and soul, appealed to Gide. "Only the glow matters," he wrote concerning the death of Madeleine and the purity of his love for her.

but Ellis put her finger on my eyelids, and when I opened my eyes, I could no longer see anything except her.

"Urien! Urien, sad brother! You who have always dreamed only of me! Remember the games we once played. Why did you have the urge in a moment of boredom to chase after my fortuitous image? You must have known that that was neither the time nor the place to possess. I await you beyond time, where the snows are eternal; we shall have crowns of snow, not garlands of flowers. Your voyage will come to an end, my brother. Never look toward the past. There are still other lands, lands which you have never known and will never know. What would it have availed you to know them? For each the route is unique and each route leads to God. But it is not from this life that your eyes can see His glory. You spoke cruel words to the poor child whom you mistook for me—and how could you have made that mistake? Then you abandoned her. She was not alive; you created her; now you must wait for her; for she could not ascend alone to the city of God. Oh! I wanted us, both of us, to take the starry route, together, alone, to the pure lights. You must guide the other one. Both of you will complete your voyage; but this end is not the true one; nothing achieves completion, my brother, except in God; be not dismayed, therefore, if you think that you are on the verge of death. Behind one heaven is another; behind all of them is God. Beloved brother, hold fast to your Hope."

Then, bending over, she wrote on the snow in glowing letters words which I, kneeling, was able to read:

THEY HAVE NOT YET OBTAINED WHAT GOD HAD PROMISED THEM—THAT ONLY IN COMPANY WITH US SHOULD THEY REACH PERFECTION.[1]

I wanted to speak to her, to ask her to speak to me at greater length, and I reached out toward her; but in the dead of night she pointed to the aurora and, rising slowly like an angel laden with prayers again set out on the seraphic route. As she rose her dress changed into a nuptial gown; I saw that it was fastened with jeweled pins; it glittered with stones; and although their brilliancy was such that it might have consumed my eyelashes, I did not feel the searing heat because of the celestial sweetness that flowed from her outstretched hands. She no longer looked toward me; I saw her ascending higher and higher; she reached the glowing gates; she was about to disappear behind a cloud. . . . Then a much whiter light dazzled me and when the cloud parted, I saw angels. Ellis was in their midst, but I could not recognize her; each angel, with upraised arms, was shaking what I had mistaken for the aurora—a curtain that had again been lowered in front of immortal flashes of light; each flame was a veil through which shone the Light. Great flashes escaped through the fringes—but when the

[1] Hebrews 11:39-40. Gide's note.

angels pulled aside the curtain, such a cry rent the skies that I covered my eyes with my hand and fell prostrate with terror.

When I arose again, night had closed in once more; in the distance I heard the voice of the sea. When I returned to the huts, I found my companions still asleep; I lay down near them, overcome by sleep.

Journey toward the pole. The excessive whiteness of things produces a strange glow; they are bathed in radiance. The wind blows furiously, and the snow, lifted up and driven by the wind, scatters, piles up, whirls, undulates, furls as cloth or human hair. One obstacle after another along the route made our journey very slow; we had to cut our way through the ice, chiseling stairs as we advanced. I do not wish to speak of our labors; they were so painful, so hard that I would seem to be complaining if I merely recounted them. Nor do I wish to speak of either the cold or our suffering; it would be ridiculous to say, "We suffered terribly," for our suffering was immeasurably greater than anything these words might suggest. I would never succeed in conveying through words the supreme bitterness of our suffering; I would never be able to explain how the very acridity of our suffering gave birth to something resembling joy, pride; nor the rabid bite of the cold.

Far to the north towered a strange rampart of ice; an enormous and prismatic block stood there like a wall. Leading up to it was a deep ravine into which spilled a whirling mass of snow, driven perhaps by an unwavering wind. Without the ropes that linked us to each other, we would have been buried in the snow. Soon we were so tired of walking through the storm that, in spite of the danger of lying down on the snow, we stretched out to sleep. We took shelter behind a big block of ice; the wind blew the snow overhead; the wall formed a grotto. We were lying on the bed of the sled and on the skin of the slaughtered reindeer.

While the other six were sleeping, I went out alone from the grotto to see if it had stopped snowing. Through the shroud of snow I thought I saw Ellis, pensive near a white rock. She seemed not to see me; she was looking toward the pole; her hair was loose, and the wind was blowing it across her face. I dared not speak to her because she seemed so sad, and I doubted that it was she. And as I was unable to be sad and to finish the voyage at the same time, I left her and went back to sleep.

The snow is now flying over our heads because of the very violence of the wind. We are at the foot of a great wall. A strange passageway leads there. The wall, as smooth as a mirror and as transparent as crystal is depressed at the end of the passageway. One spot where no snow has fallen is also transparent. Bending under the weight of our presentiments, we read these two words, written on the wall as if by a diamond on glass and reminiscent of a voice from the grave:

and then a blurred date.

And under these words we saw, after we had fallen on our knees in a common gesture—we saw a corpse lying inside the transparent ice. Settling all around him, the ice had entombed him, and the intense cold inside his sepulcher had prevented decomposition. His features betrayed frightful fatigue. He held a paper in his hand.

We felt that we had come almost to the end of our voyage; we still felt strong enough, however, to climb down the frozen wall, suspecting all the while that our goal lay beyond but not knowing for sure. And now that we had done everything possible to reach it, we found it almost futile to persevere. Before this un- known tomb we remained still on our knees impassive, unreflective, for we had reached the point where com- passion turns to self-pity and where sadness must be ignored if strength is to be conserved. The heart is emboldened only through induration. And for these reasons, rather than to avoid violating the sepulcher, we did not break through the ice despite our desire to read what was written on the paper held by the corpse. After a short prayer we stood up and began painfully to climb up the wall of ice.

I am not sure how the wind that caused the storm arose, for as soon as we had crossed over the wall, it ceased and the atmosphere became almost mild. The other side of the wall was a gentle declivity formed by soft snow. Then there was a row of vegetation; then a small unfrozen lake. I think that the surrounding wall was perfectly circular, for the slopes tapered regularly, and since the wind no longer blew inside this enclosed area, the water in the lake remained calm.

We were sure that this was the end; we could no longer advance; but knowing that we would not know what to do there if we went down to the shore, in order to contrive some sort of conclusion, or some culminating gesture, we had the pious notion of going back to get the unknown corpse and burying it beside the lake. For we thought that this traveler, too, another person had also traveled far to see the lake, and we were sorry that he had been unable to reach his goal.

We went back to his tomb, broke through the ice and removed his body. When we tried to read the paper which he was holding, however, we saw that it was completely blank. Our disappointment was all the more painful because our curiosity had been dissipated. We carried his body to the little polar shore without ever putting into words our feeling that it was better perhaps for him never to have seen the anticipated shore and for the wall to have separated him from his goal during his lifetime, for even if the facts had been different the words chiseled on his tomb would probably have been the same.

A cheerless dawn was breaking as we made one last attempt to blot out our misgivings by digging a grave in the grass between the snow and the water in the lake.

We no longer wished to return to the regions where flowers bloomed more profusely, to the monotonous past, for one does not travel backward and downward to find life. If we had known at the outset that this was what we had come to see, perhaps we would not have started; that is why we gave thanks to God for having hidden from us the goal and for having withheld it from us until our efforts to attain it had afforded us some pleasure, the only certain pleasure; and we also thanked God because our intense suffering had made us hope for a splendid end.

We would have liked indeed to devise anew some tenuous and more pious hope; having satisfied our pride and feeling that the fulfillment of our destinies no longer depended on us, we now waited for the things around us to become a little more faithful to us.

Kneeling still, we probed the black water for the reflection of the heaven of my dreams.

END

ENVOY

Madame! I deceived you:
We undertook no voyage.
We beheld no gardens
or pink flamingos beside the sea;
it was not to us that sirens
beckoned with their hands.
If I ate not the fruits,
and slept not under the trees;
if I kissed not the hands
of perfumed Haïatalneful;
if I believed in tomorrows;
if I recounted these deeds;
then they were but mirages,
then they were but phantoms.
I think that I would have resisted; I waited;
But temptations never came to me.
Ellis! Forgive me! I lied.
This voyage is but my dream,
we never left the confines
of the chamber of our thoughts,—
and we passed through life
without ever seeing it. We read.

You would come in the morning
exhausted from your prayers.
Madame, I deceived you:
This whole book is but a lie.
But I did not shout,
for a dreamer is calm.
One day, however, as you know,
I wanted to look at life;
we studied the world about us.
But I found the things of this world
so serious, so terrible,
so responsible on all sides,
that I dared not speak the truth;
I turned away—oh! Madame—forgive me;
I preferred to tell a lie.
I was afraid of shouting too loudly
and destroying poetry
if I had told the Truth,
the Truth that must be heard;
I preferred still to lie
and to wait,—wait, wait . . .*

La Roque, Summer, 1892.

* In another place (Journal, 1930) Gide stated, "I write only
for those who can read between the lines." The turning away may
refer to a crucial episode in the life of the author—his discovery
that Madeleine, far from being serene and unapproachable, was
apprehensive and in need of his protection; Madeleine, after dis-
covering that her mother had a lover, suffered in silence. Gide
took it upon himself to guide her, and have her share his in-
terests in nature, literature and philosophy.